Copyright

This book is a work of fiction. Names, characters, businesses, places and events are either a product of the authors' imagination or are used fictitiously. Artistic license has been taken with the geography of some locations. Any resemblance to actual persons, living or dead, events or locales, are entirely coincidental.

Front cover photograph courtesy of Mike Bolam.

http://www.flickr.com/photos/landscapy/

Biography photograph courtesy of Ian Michael Bray.

http://bleepthewhat.tumblr.com/

Kindle publishing code: A1JJAW9LIVIQIP

For Mim: shine on…

…and for Rani, Jonathon, Katy B, Lily Ann and Alexander, with love.

Table of Contents

Prologue

These days are cold and I am tired of searching. Tired of seeking. It was better when there was another. I wonder what will happen, what will I find. Who will find me? I am reminded of old tales, of a thousand years of watching. A thousand years of waiting. I drift through time, moving like water.

Chapter 1

Reflection – *an image formed by reflection, a sign, serious thought.*

'...Time (The Revelator)'

Perhaps I am being unfair. After all, the mornings are spectacular. Sunrise spreads like a promise, golden and blue, and stay-up-late-stars twinkle and finally fade, beaten by a greater light. Night rolls away. Day breaks. Edinburgh is bleak in November and it always seems the hardest month. I don't know why. It is impossible to stay outside for long and the very bones of me are cold. I can contrive to remain indoors for days and days. Socks in bed. Tense little bodies. Three jumpers.

It's funny; you'd think January would be the 'difficult' month. But January is always full of New Year resolutions that, mainly, I keep. A new start. Suddenly I'm sprung forward into the future. January seems to fly by! January has that faint promise of summer. Ahead and glittering in the distance, even though it's going to be a long while before spring brings all those rushing, blushing greens, unfolding promises, and wild roving winds. For now we are stuck, mainly, with the low, keening winter blues.

November.

And *'...These dreams of you...'*

Later that afternoon I walk down Marchmont Road and across The Meadows. The streets are quiet, it's only 4pm but already the yellow light is fading from the sky. Venus is rising and the late afternoons darkening light is tinged with banks of low orange cloud. I walk past windows steamed up with cosy, inside lives. A bleak wind sliding of the Firth of Forth is biting at my neck and I can smell winter in the air; its leading edge is sharp and clear. I walk on through George Square to the Old Town. I'm very happy to get to Black Bo's and delighted, as ever, to find it earlyevening, quiet and gentle. Our city never stops attracting backpackers and tourists, even in November they come. They are drawn here, pulled by the Scots fearsome reputation as welcoming hosts. To my right is the dormant volcano and the dark jagged line of Salisbury crags; both rise out of the city centre parkland like an impossible dream. Edinburgh; seat of ancient Kings, our Athens of the North is beautiful, grand and steeped in bloody political and social history. At this time of day tourists are still milling around on the Royal Mile in the half light, seeking pieces of history to take away home and searching for their links to ancestors. They are caught between the Castle and the Palace, the new Parliament: Scotland's disgrace, and the tat shops, the whisky tastings, the ubiquitous Australian street performers and the fearsome skirl of the pipers. Most folk don't realise they are listening to weapons of war, musical instruments that are designed to freeze the blood, creating anxiety in their discordant and oppressive din. That's why we all need the whisky.

I am meeting Delilah, though she's not really called that. She made Delilah up for herself in the late 80's and it stuck. I am envious. I've tried all my life to get a new name. It started my first day at school. Aged five I tried, and since then I've never really given up trying. My problem is I don't know what I should be called so it's hard to convince anyone else. It's an indication of my general state of inertia, of not knowing. Nada. Now't. Nought. Nu*think*. It's a good indication of the confusion, the never quite settling, the grass-may-be-greener feeling, that follows most of us disconnected, alienated, displaced, and disenchanted, lonely, godless souls around. Maybe what I really desire is to be able to buy a new name every year. Try it on for a while and see what it does to me; For Me. Try it on for a year and find out how much of the name is made by the person and how much by outside perception of what a name like David or Violet means. Nature / Nurture. It could be whole new science. Ein Stein.

So Delilah is late, she always is. I wish I could be late. I can't. Not even when I know the person I'm meeting with will, themselves, be late. Tick tock. Delilah and I are a unity of opposites; we have opposing tendencies. It is innate, the knowledge that opposites are necessary for the world, for our balance. I remember my philosophy lecturer fixing us all with a baleful eye, his disdain for us evident in the shake of his large grey head and his crippling sarcasm. Three hundred and fifty students held in his gaze while he enlightened; "*without contradiction there could be no reality. Reality itself is inherently unstable.*" For sure, this is two and a half thousand year old thinking, but never more apt than in this modern twenty-first century world. Tick and Tock. The Western mind has an obsession with clocks that many think began with nineteenth century industrialisation. Actually, it began with Galileo in the early sixteen hundreds when he discovered the principle of the pendulum. Galileo also discovered that bodies fall at the same velocity, no matter the weight of the body. This velocity accelerates at a comforting thirty two feet per second, per thirty two feet. I think perhaps he came up with this theory as he tried to envisage the best way to deal with his detractors. Thanks to the pendulum we have;

Railway time, present time, unified time, time in the mind versus time on the clock; a moment to me; a life time to you. The urge to, always, keep moving. Tick Tock. Time exists in three dimensions; the past, the present and the future. In all these states it is subjective in its influence and its meaning, and the worn, frayed, tangled rope of memory connects the three. In us all exists the past, the present and the future. Temporal temporality.

'...And we run and we run to catch up with the sun, but it's sinking, racing around to come up behind you again. The sun is the same in a relative way but you're older, shorter of breath and one day closer to death...'

Delilah says she grew up in the Solomon Islands, on San Cristobal. The only daughter of two English teachers, she has a wild, windblownsea Pacific Ocean feel about her. Delilah has a quick quiet smile and is a great storyteller, but only when the mood takes her, which is rare. Tall, athletic and rangy with weathered salty tasting skin, and unkempt wild, shoulder length sandy hair. She has incredible eyes; grey flecked with gold, set deep into hooded lids, and overarched with thick eyebrows. She has many sides. Delilah knew me before I knew David and she likes to remind me how different life was then. Although I still wanted a different name. And time still tick tocked. We were certainly young, of that there can be no doubt but I struggle to remember much else that was different. My rope is frayed and knotted. However, Delilah can see a memory across a void of twenty years and relay all details in glorious Technicolor. Coloured memories. Maybe it's just that mine are black and white. She sees across a void I see across and avoid. There are a few years missing between us. There was that time she went off the radar in the late 1980s. She came back with her long hair shorn, too thin by far and a look of loss, a fading of the gold that flecked her eyes. That was when she changed her name; perhaps it stuck because she really was changed herself.

Delilah and I lived together for years, off and on during our twenties. Students in student-ridden

Marchmont and attending Edinburgh University. I studied all sorts; Politics, Philosophy, Art and Literature. She studied Medicine. All the thoughts and somebody thought to remember to write it all down. Bless the writer. Bless the thinker. Bless the healer. Blessed be. I'm still waiting to graduate. Too much thinking. It's another one of those never quite finished things. Tock Tick. I seem to have been a part -time student for ever and for my sins I still live in student ridden Marchmont, where the streets ring late at night with tiny drunken dramas. My tenement stair neighbours and myself are regularly woken to the sound of loud 4am inconsideration: of-key gang singing, best achieved arm in arm, while listing to the left and then to the right. The clack of high heels lurching along the middle of cobbled streets, the sandstone buildings ringing with echoes, laughter and occasional despair. We, the stupidly sober, stumble bleary eyed through our days, tired and, ultimately despairing of the Yoof. Delilah got out.

Delilah finally rushes in with the North wind on her tail and in her winter clothes and while motioning drink up signs at me goes straight to the bar. She orders two single malts and smiles with gratitude at Bernie as he snuggles her face in his big warm paws and then hands her the water of life. She pays for the drinks and comes across the tiny bar to greet me. She flops down and removes some of her outer clothes, "BRRR!!! Chilly!" she whispers. I grin back at her and sip my Cardhu, "slainte!"

When I first met Delilah she was roughly about eighteen. As I've said my rope is frayed. She was really beautiful, like all girls are at that age, with their smooth skin, inner glow and bright eyes. The innocence of youth. So attractive to the other innocents. The other youth. To the older folks they seem frivolous and daft and full of convictions that can never stand the test of time. They believe they are eternal flames and as such will never die, will never fade. Will never grow cold. It always surprises me because surely they are surrounded by other such evidence. Here I am in front of you. Tick.

She is still beautiful, although the years have taken much from her. I have noticed how she has become invisible. People used to pay attention when she walked down the street. Now they don't see her. She has become one of the Others. The evidence. Tock. Some days I hate Delilah. There are other days I love Delilah too much and I am very, very afraid. I think that some days Delilah is afraid too, but for different reasons. She never actually says it out loud, but there is something in the flick of her eyes and the way she listens ever so carefully to some quiet inner voice. Her head slightly to one side and a middle distance look in her eyes. I want to remind her at times like this that she really should be keeping her eyes focused and on the present. Her danger may sneak up when she is watching that middle distance. I wonder where she goes. I wonder what it is she fears. Maybe I shouldn't wonder, after all, we now live in The Paradigm of Prevention. The! High! State! Of! Alert! We! Live! On! Alert for things that never happen. Afraid of being afraid. Afraid of fear.

'...How could it have come to this, I'm really worried about living...'

Chapter 2

Re-fraction - *of water, air or glass, makes a ray of light change direction when it enters at an angle*

Normally I wake up slowly. Some days I don't wake till late and then I'm a little confused, a bit displaced, I am lost in time. It may take me a whole day to catch up to myself. Sometimes I'm lost completely, cast adrift on a sea of particle exchange I become part of Capras Dance of Shiva. Today I wake at 7am, and the icy-fingery-pink-tipped-dawn finds me boarding the Glasgow train from Edinburgh Waverly. The train still smells of Friday night people; excitement, stale perfume and booze. It's filthy. I put my bag on the seat next to me, a strong message to Others; Do Not Sit Here – this seat has been bagged. We leave Waverly Station, pulling out under the shadow of the towering Castle rock, clacking slowly through Princes Street Gardens, trees bare and stark. The cold morning already darkening and paralysing even the birdsong.

I doze across the dreary central belt, ignoring the slack heaps and worn out industry, and wake at Glasgow Queen Street. I grab a coffee from the frozen vendor, we smile at each other, a moment of common understanding, as our winter breaths meet and mingle, and then I board the rickety old train that will take me up the West Highland Line to Mallaig. At Crainlaroch the train splits and woe-be-tide any fool who has fallen asleep at the wrong end. You are now headed to Oban my friend and unless you plan to jump off and walk back, you really are heading to Oban my friend. It's not a mistake people tend to make twice. I didn't.

I am amused, as always, to see the train has come from somewhere else; somewhere in Yorkshire. Trans-Pennine Railways it sheepishly declares. It has been retired to Scotland, to move slowly, slowly, ever so slowly across the landscape. The train chuffs across the loneliness of Rannoch Moor; small black peaty lochs, reflecting dark skies, hiding secrets in unknown depths. They always remind me of Frodo and the companions journey towards Mordor. The moor stretches to the horizon, lochs, heather and peat, huge skies hang low and oppressive and as far as the eye can see. It never fails to diminish me; somehow, for all its beauty it appears exaggerated and overdone. A parody of a Scottish moor. We creep round the back of the fearsome sentinels of Glencoe, like a thief in broad daylight, and on, through the remaining stands of the Caledonian Forest.

The motion of the train lulls me and I begin to doze. I dream of the Birnam Oak. I am sleeping inside its hollow trunk, the dark night sky hidden from me by dense bark and history. A soft voice speaks to me through the darkness, through time, and tells me the oak is a thousand years old. So far, the oak is standing tall, against the passage of a million-billion-moments. Every moment a micro-dot in the trees long history. There will be nation in mourning if it is toppled, or when the rot sets in, as it must surely in old age. These days the oak is propped up by large crutches, a younger tree cut down utilitarian like to serve the greater good, the longer life perhaps, or perhaps they are pieces of itself, chopped off to offer solace. The rattling and jerking of the train wakes me and, momentarily, I cannot remember who I am.

I love the West Highland Line and relish the hours ahead of me as the train creeps across the ancient land. The vegetation is all shades of brown at this time of year and I strain the landscape for glimpses of elusive and highly camouflaged brown and grey deer. My eyes seek out solitary stags pursuing hinds, all moving to lower pastures to find better grazing for the winter months. The stags rut during September to November, losing the red in their coats and fighting for wives and the right to territory, their massive 16 point antlers loud and fierce weapons. These beasts, the largest of our land mammals have been here for over 11,000 years. Roaming wild across the glens, they are now also farmed, and culled as a sport for the rich. They still feed us and keep us warm. The site of a stag, proud and, to all intents, free, fills my heart. My belly also rumbles.

The day has brightened as we head North West. It's now a sky blue day but very windy, nearly gale force. I wonder if there will be a boat. A few clouds are scudding overhead like a runaway bride, her veil trailing far behind her, as if reluctant to give up the dream of being

M r s.

I can feel the wind buffeting the train and roaring drafts come at me through the cracks in the doors. We slowly pick up speed and chuff across the viaduct at Glenfinnan. The monument, built in 1815, still stands tall in Glenfinnan, a stark fairy tale tower at the northern head of Loch Sheil, reminding those who pass by and care to look, and care to see, that history was made here: Bonnie Prince Charlie came ashore in a wee open boat from France in 1745 and gathered the clans: MacDonald's, Cameron's, McPhees and MacDonnell's, all in the name of his father – James Stuart: The Old Pretender, and the rights of Scotland as an independent nation. He stayed a while, waiting, waiting, waiting, till he had raised enough of an army to challenge, and attempt to take back, his family's right to take the throne. He and the Clans made the beginnings of the Jacobite rebellion, a challenge which ended in disaster eight months later at The Battle of Culloden. Scotland has waited since, waited for a chance to seize back its independence, holding fast to its own legal and education system. It's close now, this independence. So very close and it will come. But three hundred odd years are a long time to be married and the divorce when it comes, will be messy. Of that there can be no doubt.

As we pass alongside Glenfinnan I salute old friends, those ladies of the loch side. I remember those who knew kitchen table ways; there was always 'A Highland Welcome', front doors without keys, friendship and understanding. These would always be waiting for me. I would sing a song in return for my supper, my storytelling valued and treasured and I in turn would treasure the care extended to me. This care would create the need to create, beautifully circular and true in its being: listen, write, sing or tell it to listeners, then listen and write, creating our mutual histories.

Onward we creep. As we pass Glenuig, hidden from me by the brown and gold mountains, but laying there over the water nevertheless, I salute again, silently, and fall backwards in time. I'm spinning through years of hazy memories to village hall ways; finer days; halcyon days. Warm summer nights spent skinny dipping in the sea. Drinking as the brightness dimmed slightly in the west, a moment or two only it seemed, before the light from the east would begin the day again. We didn't sleep much then, midsummer created an energy that fed us, we were fed by light and sunshine. These were times when we all thought we could live forever. Could live together. And Christ, were we not oh so beautiful and oh so brave?

I can see you clearly. You are radiant. You are smiling back at me as we try to Strip the Willow. I was terrible at the more formal East Coast Dances, with their strict tempos and careful sets. Somehow the steps never got fixed in my brain. I did a bit better with the west coast ceilidh, where the musicians would feel the atmosphere in the room and play accordingly, intent on spinning the dancers faster and faster. I loved the Boston Two Step and the Gay Gordon's, two person dances that enabled a holding, a closeness and a shared intimacy. These dances enabled an opportunity to be held by stronger arms and sometimes, to be surprised... Somehow though, I always created havoc on the floor amongst the whirling crowd in the larger sets. And always, always, I was mighty relieved when it was time to play our set and we would move people in a different way. You were always a little more crazy when we were on the west coast and the deeper, truer self of you, would come blazing through. The-displaced-Trans-Pennine-train-moves-slowly-on-towards-

Arisaig. I feel bonded to the train, purely by the virtue of both of us being where we don't belong.

At Arisaig, my heart is sore from receiving postcards from the edge of my mind. I try to shake off the past and so look further to the west, to the future and the Isle of Eigg. An Sgurr, at its centre, surfs the horizon, rising impossibly tall, an exposed pitchstone ridge and the largest of its kind in Europe. Famous and infamous, Eigg is the place where the devolved Scottish Parliament first placed our hopes and our aspirations. Community Buy Outs began here and the days of absentee landlords, who bought titles and shirked responsibility through the twentieth century, began their long awaited decline. Eigg: my spiritual home, my place of worship. Ultimately, I hope, my final resting place. However, although the Small Isles call and pull me, and Laigg Bay and her people tug at my soul, I'm actually on my way to Knoydart. It's been over twenty years since I last set foot in Knoydart. I think of you and wish you were here to remind me. What did we do?

David has been living in Knoydart on and off for over twenty years. He arrived first in Edinburgh twenty four years ago, seeking respite from the depths of a sad and dirty Southern England. He stayed a while, stayed till we couldn't do without him. Until his branches and leaves, if not his roots, were entwined with ours. Then he pulled them up, and carrying them he walked the sixteen miles overland, arriving in Knoydart with his canoe on his back. In his canoe was his life. And also some of ours.

Of course, in a perfect world boat and train would be supportive of each other and plan to meet. But time and tide don't work together; tides being natural; movable and fixed only by the action of the moon. Time is fixed by Time, and, apart from that sudden bi yearly sixty minute leap forward and back, and February's four yearly 29th day, Time, tick, tock's, on, at, a, reg-ul-ar, reg-ul-at-d, uni-form, thanks, to, Gal, i, le, o, pen-du-lum, swing. The train arrives after the boat has gone. I alight in Mallaig at

6pm into the bracing, salty winter darkness and prepare to sit out the cold night until tomorrow.

Mallaig: a fisherman's town, a working town, it was once the fishing capital of the West Coast of Scotland and it is in no way bonnie. The ice factory looms over the harbour. The squalling winds rattle and thrum through the halyards and the stink of fish is high on the blustery air. The council estate on the hill, which faces the harbour, reinforces the working man atmosphere. I can hear a dog barking in the distance and close by the lonely sound of the sea slapping at the harbour walls and at the hulls of moored fishing boats. *The Loch Nevis,* the roll-on-roll-off ferry that services both the Small Isles and the Isle of Skye during the winter months is berthed for the night and her safety lights on the bridge cast a cold light. She is named after the loch I will travel up tomorrow. I have a deep fondness for these vessels, our lives depend on their ship shape state through all manner of weather and I have taken countless journeys back and forth across the minches, trusting crews to deliver us all safely. I have stood solitary and windblown on the deck, searching the waters for the secret life underneath. I have leaned over the prow, where the public aren't allowed, and watched pods of dolphins fly alongside us, racing our bow wave. I have held communion with a Minky Whale as she swam away in the opposite direction, her tale graceful and full, waving to my gaze for many nautical miles. Out across the water I can see the lighthouse at Ardnamurchen, signalling across the most westerly point in the British Isles, keeping the sea farers safe as they negotiate the Minches. I always wonder what tourists must think alighting in Mallaig. What a possible disappointment the wee town could be after the journey along the Road to the Isles, which is full of promises and stunning views. Mallaig. I head for the pub.

Chapter 3

Reduction – *the action of reducing something, a smaller picture or photograph*

'...I remember, holding on to you, all those long and lonely nights you put me through...sometimes, I break down and cry, but I can't remember if we said goodbye...'

David is standing at the long picture window, his angular body is tense, and he is gazing with dark eyes at the grey and angry sea. White horses are racing the wind toward the battered shoreline and he wonders if the boat will come after all. There is rain in the air and the tattered clouds race each other towards the south west, stretching away from him and out to sea. They are layered grey, white, silver and mauve beneath blue skies. He watches the gulls flying in low and banking, marvelling, as always, at their ability to stay on the wing, almost in spite of themselves. He notices the Sea Eagle is absent and wonders, not for the first time, what he himself portends in the signs he see's around him. The word on the wing is that the boat is bringing his life back. A piece long missing may now fit. It may not. He sighs and turns away from the long view. He turns inward, towards a warmer place.

The sea is November-rough and soon I'm hanging on for dear life. My arms and shoulders are aching from bracing and my arse is sore from banging it as we hit the bottom of the troughs. The boat is tiny and quiet, no tourists, only the essential or those dedicated to homecoming are travelling today. It's one of those uncertain days. A boat? Knoydart, so remote. There is no road to attach it, umbilical like, to the infrastructure of Scotland, and so a community which is a sixteen mile walk overland, depends on the boat as much as the Islands it gazes across the water at. Rum rises, magnificently purple and grey and its Cuillins, stark and sharp against the sky, tower over the water and a sheer drop down to the rocky shore.

They seem to lean towards Eigg, towards the striped silver and black sands of Laigg Bay and the tiny village of Cleadale. Knoydart watches from out of Loch Nevis; straining for a peep of Muck as she nestles deeper into the sea behind Eigg. Two thousand people once lived on the Knoydart peninsula, wrestling a life out of land and sea. The last three hundred and thirty two of these were cleared in 1853 to make way for sheep and forestry. Folks snatched and herded from all they had ever known and shipped across the world aboard the *Sillan* to Canada, to live or die. The people have returned to Knoydart over the years, slowly though and in fewer numbers. They are once more wrestling a life out of the land and sea, the tourism keeps Scotland afloat.

Finally the boat docks and I search the tiny slipway for any familiar faces in the small crowd that has gathered to meet the boat. It is always emotional. Sometimes very subtle, sometimes overwhelming, this meeting of ferry and land. People meet people; the journeying and the journeyed too. The small communities on the west coast are far flung but deeply connected and you can never tell who may be where, as folks follow the work and trade skills from community to community, building houses, or working the forestry and the seas. The boat is here. What will the boat bring? Essential supplies and sometimes surprises. Today the boat has brought me. I hear a shout and a laugh and suddenly I am surrounded by loving folk who are wrapped in yellow oil skins. They hug me and kiss me and tell me it's great to have me back. I'm literally whirled off my feet and before I know it we are all in the pub and I'm surrounded by the chat and the banter of folks who know one another well, too well sometimes. It's good to be back amongst it, to be part of it, and after the anonymity of the city a welcome respite to be in the company of those who are deeply connected. But I wonder, who am I now. Who has come back?

Emmylou Harris is singing Steve Earl on the jukebox; '*...was I just off somewhere or maybe just too high? Cause I can't remember, if we said* *goodbye. Goodbye…'* Her voice, sublime, could always make me cry and I come to myself suddenly with the roar of pub noise back in my ears and tears making my eyes too wide and myself too, too blue. I push my way past the wave of oilskins and the smell of boat oil, diesel and hard graft. Past the smokers huddled round the door, like mammoth, greedy moths from a distance past. I push on through the blue acrid haze that's formed around the doorway and finally I'm in the quiet, clear outside. I head for the shoreline, the machair is soft and yielding beneath my feet and I am on the edge of the saltspraysea. The Atlantic Ocean pounds the lochshore, pushed hard by the wind, as the wide, dark night sky watches. The sea is boiling and foaming as it keeps it secrets, its treasures and those it has claimed for itself. It always has pulled at me. Spoken to me in quiet underwater whispers and I think I may see my end, and my beginning in those dark and stormy waters. As the selkies sing, I hear them again, they call to me and they speak of a life underneath. I hunker down on the machair, sheltering from the seaspray and pulling my jacket close to keep out the wind. As my tears dry on my face I feel overwhelmed by the great sea and its depths, overwhelmed by my own secrets, hidden from me. Our national bard springs suddenly to my mind and my favourite of his poems comes unbidden;

When Deaths dark stream I ferry over,
A time that surely shall come.
In heaven itself I will ask no more,
Than just a Highland Welcome.

As I gaze out across the wild concealed ocean the picture I paint in my head is clear; a lavender room, the smell of carbolic. Seasons are frozen and stretched. I remember a place far away in space and time, another lifetime perhaps. My life? A half life? These questions pull at me. They find me in the deep dark night and I awake with fright gasping for breath and searching anxiously around my familiar Edinburgh bedroom for the perceived invader. The shadows cast by plants become demons that have every right to haunt me. The mirror-ball, which hangs in the window, reveals a thousand lives. It is an eye, looking for another eye. The long picture on the far wall becomes a jagged tooth searching for another tooth. Where is the threat? Is it my own self? Do others wake like me, fearful, short of breath and misconstruing all the familiar shapes in a familiar room? Am I the only one?

The lavender room. Outside that room waited another sky. A vaulted sky, different in every way from the wide-and-dark-one which watches over me now. My questions drive me forward; they have brought me this far anyway. I hurt myself at times in my effort to think and too often I end up remembering; '*the supreme paradox of thought is the attempt to discover something thought cannot think.*' Are my searching questions a paradox of thought, something that thought cannot think? Or is it simply that there are no answers. Or, are these simply the wrong questions.

The low *A* on the fiddle is a haunting and melancholic note. It pulls me back inside the crowded pub. I'm engulfed by the tunes and that melancholic *A*. I can hear echoes of the past in that drone. As I try to find my place once more in the crowded noisy bar I realise with sharp relief that I have not been missed. Despite the Highland Welcome afforded me, folks have returned, for the most part, to their own busy lives. Arguing and laughing, teasing and flirting. Drinking. I find a quieter corner and sit, watching the room and the many stories unfolding, which run in and around each other, parallel and in flux. Opposite and united. In my wandering thoughts I find Greek myths; the nymph Echo was one of Narcissus' many lovers. She lost her voice, and through the centuries since has only be heard in her repetition of others. Echo was punished by Hera because Echo entertained her with long stories while Zeus's concubines, the mountain nymphs, escaped Hera's jealous eye. The nymph Echo can still be heard in Scottish glens and across Scottish waters, and in everyone's life there is an echo of that echo. Like the after light that burns your retina from a camera flash. Is that me…me…me… or maybe that's you…maybe it's you. It's you. You.

Chapter 4

Remembrance – *a thing kept or given as a reminder of someone*

'....I'm sitting here burning daylight thinking about the past...'

I have been thinking of the future. However, I can't reflect on the future without thinking about the past and I have become lost in time, considering how much of the present day is taken up with past and future. Tock. Remembrance is a slippery business; we colour our memories with our knowledge of the present, and how the past has affected the decisions we made. The present affects our decisions retrospectively. We wish to be worthier, to see ourselves in the best light possible and we reinvent ourselves accordingly. As each minute passes we see life differently from how others around us see it. Witnesses will always tell a different tale about an event. Investigators are suspicious if all the stories match up too closely because, quite simply, they shouldn't; everyone's perception makes a different reality. Perspective. Subjective.

Again in my black and white memory I see a teacher; a lecture hall and anxious students striving for understanding. Several are simply clockwatching and proving again, and again, and again, that time on the clock and time in the mind are a lifetime apart. I have been that student; time hangs, the clock does not move, and outside in the fresh air of the park and in the chaotic city, life flies by at a million miles an hour. So many moments of living missed while listening to explanations of how we live.

I'm unsure when it happened. I remember Delilah coming back from wherever it was that she'd disappeared to for over a year. She was too thin and had cut her long hair very short. She was really different somehow, perceptibly changed to her core. That's when she changed her name. I guess that was in the late 1980s. I remember watching her sleeping, restlessly dreaming, then her waking up crying and I was there, waiting, in the half light.

"Hey it's ok, it's just a dream."

"Jesus!" She exclaimed sitting up. "Whatthehell! No, oh,"

Delilah fell back to the bed, like a wave defeated by greedy and absorbent sandy shore, she moaned.

"Go back to sleep." I advised softly.

"Shit!" she sat up again. Folded her knees up to her chest and wrapping her arms around her long legs, she dropped her head and began to cry softly.

"What's wrong my pal?" I asked. All hell broke loose. She was up and spitting at me, her cropped hair all bed-head and her gold-flecked-eyes flashing. She looked, for all the world, like a cornered mountain-cat-girl.

"Get out! Get out! Get out! Get out of here!" She came at me then with her arms windmilling and her long nails scratching. Jesus! I'd never seen her like this before. I fled from her, from her rage. Was she mad? Had she forgotten?

I found myself down by the Shore in Leith village, feeling strange and lost. Edinburgh, normally familiar and comforting, like the smells of home and the shape of your own bed, like old friends and your best cosy jumper, had the quality of a dream. The light from the neon city was muted by the Haar blowing in off the Firth of Forth. The streets and water side oddly empty of people. There was no-one close by, but in the distance I could hear the sounds of the night, the clicking of high heels, an altercation somewhere. Someone else laughing with someone else. I couldn't remember where I lived. I couldn't seem to remember much. I was surprised by the temperature. It was the middle of the night and warm, balmy even, despite the Haar which normally chills everything, leaving wet prints on all as it blows visibly down the street. Desperately confused I walked around, making no sense of anything, till I found myself back at Delilah's door.

I rang the buzzer. No answer. I rang again. The lights are on in her flat, the curtains are drawn and the glow through them is warm and comforting. It seemed natural to fish the key out from under the mat and so I let myself in, like I'd done a thousand times before. I unlocked the door to the flat and found Delilah staring at the middle distance, eyes seeing far beyond the walls of her cramped flat. She was nursing a Glenfiddich, the open bottle by her side, it was nearly empty. She didn't even look up when I went in. I sat down opposite her. She was crying again, rocking herself, her hands fluttering around her face in agitated desperation. I crossed the room and this time she let me hold her. Time stopped for a while and a certain peace spread through us. A kindness. Suddenly though, without warning, she became cold and hard in my arms. Something changed in her, a splitting, a wrenching, an understanding. She pulled away from me violently and looked at me hard, straight at me, as though seeing me properly for the first time. Her eyes were deep dark water, and, oh so lonely, and then she asked “how did you?” Somehow, I know exactly what she means and answer her quietly, “David told me.”

Chapter 5

Repulsion – *a force under the influence of which objects tend to move away from each other.*

'…and if a hundred million light years, could spiral inward and bend, if only we'd connect. It's such a long stretch of time.'

When I met David I was about twenty four. He would have been about thirty five I suppose, and I thought he was the most beautiful man I had ever seen: 5 foot 9, with dark straight hair. Angular body. If you looked at him a certain way he was very handsome, too handsome in fact. At other times you wondered what had made you think so because his features just didn't quite add up. It was something to do with the nose/eye ratio. His dark hair hung down over his brown eyes and he was constantly brushing it irritably aside. His hands were misplaced on his body type; you would expect such an angular person to have long tapered fingers, musical looking, artistic even. But his weren't. They sat short and crooked on his hands which were in turn small. The backs of his hands were scarred with small burns. They were a remnant from his earlier days as a fire starter, this was the explanation he gave me when I asked him about them, then infuriatingly refused to expand further. Teasing me with his mysteries. I wondered and then I had hoped that he was gay. We both loved him deeply, although we never discussed it and he seemed oblivious. He didn't seem to notice and if he did notice he didn't seem to care. We pretended not to notice that he didn't seem to care and so it became a complicit impasse that was, at the same time, both comfortable and highly uncomfortable.

I remember Australia. We were all there. The climate: so exotic, so different, so warm, wrapping around me and holding me tight, almost suffocating me. It hit me like a wall from the moment I stepped off the plane. Heat. It has its Scottish opposite, which is a cold sharp slap, drizzle, chilled bones. Tight little bodies, three jumpers. I had never been so far from home and the sky, vaulted with stars I didn't recognize, was huge and bright above me. I loved to lie on my back under the indigo warm and dark bright night, and try to work out what I was looking at. Perspective… probably one of the most useful words in any language. Subjective experience; impossible to relate.

Delilah had been gone for about 6 months. I told David I wanted to visit the coast. I hadn't mentioned Delilah. She was in Kayama, on the shoreline running between Melbourne and Sydney. We had driven across from Canberra, through all that prehistoric dry and dying, brown, bleak land to the soft, verdant, rolling coastline, pretty seaside towns and the wide blue sea. I was shocked by the state of her. She was too thin by far and had shorn her hair. Her face was pointy and sharp and she wouldn't look at me. There was a tension in her I had never felt before. I couldn't make head or tail of it and feeling awkward and teary I volunteered to go get some food in for lunch. The grey clapboard one-story house was small, unwelcoming and empty. The grey paint on its outside walls, peeling and cracked with the heat and it had an unlived in feel, its curtains were worn, torn and dirty and the cupboards were almost bare. No wonder she looked thin I thought. I stepped out onto the veranda, pushing open the fly blown screen door, the floor boards creaking under me and dust rising to choke my already tight throat. I walked on through the unkempt and dry dusty garden, to the sound of rustling creatures in the dry undergrowth. The day was typically hot, Australia hot, 35 degrees, cavernous blank blue skies stretched overhead with a bank of grey cloud threatening on the horizon; its leading edge held the promise of rain that probably would not fall. The garden gate was rusted and broken and it creaked loudly as I opened it, startling a flock of pink and grey Gallahs to flight. They wheeled above me crying geeelahhh geelaaahhh, scolding me bawdily, before they settled back into the silver Eucalyptus trees that shaded the overgrown garden, from the bush beyond the broken picket fence.

When I got back from the shops, the place was quiet. "Did you get anything tasty?" David kissed me as he asked the question, preventing me replying.

"Get off!" I laughed, adding "Yes, I got some seafood and salad. The seafood is fresh of the boat. Reminds me of the Scottish west coast, in a dreamy opposite sort of way. Look at the size of these prawns, they are three times as big as what we would get back home. Delilah looks like she needs feeding up. God knows what's going on here. Don't you think it's all a bit odd? I mean, she wasn't even pleased to see us. Hmm, David?" my voice tailed off as I realised David was standing beside me, staring at the floor, with tears rolling down his cheeks.

"My God David! What's wrong, what's happened?" I pulled him to me and held him; my head level with his, breathing in the scent of him. The smell I loved so much. Something in me, a keener sense, a tumbling lock and an intuition I didn't want, told me that David knew the answers to my questions. He wasn't telling. But he knew.

"Tell me!" I demanded. And so he did. And then his mouth was making the shapes for words but I could no longer hear them.

And I was falling.

Chapter 6

Restoration – *the returning of something to a former condition.*

'...Well someone told me yesterday, that when you give your love away, you act as if you just don't care, you look as if you're going somewhere...'

I came too in a single bed in a lavender blue room. Alone. I am thirsty, my tongue too large and numb. My eyes are gritty and swollen, my joints stiff and cracking with my movements. My back and kidneys hurt and ache as though I have spent forever in bed. It takes me an age to wake and as I drift in and out of consciousness my eyes occasionally focus on the far wall. There's a picture of a steam train crossing a viaduct in a Scottish glen. The picture is the only relief on the bare walls. My eyes are blurring and weeping with the sharp fluorescent light and it takes me forever to make sense of what I am looking at. Within the picture I think I recognize the viaduct at Glenfinnan and the shining water of Loch Shiel in the distance. The scene is autumnal, shades of November, with a sharp clear blue sky. Two stags gaze out of the picture. They stand proudly, antlers ready for battle, under the silver birch trees which dot the foreground. Three tiny clouds stand out, little dots in the blue looking for all the world like a brides trailing veil. The picture is a print of that old fashioned kind of painting normally found in an ornate gilt frame. Heavy and cumbersome in every way. Heavy with oils, tradition and heritage. Christ, I could almost smell the peat, the whisky and the heather. I could hear the Red Kites and the Sheerwaters, calling me home.

I slept once inside the Birnam Oak, the sandy floor cool and soft against me. A thousand years of endurance towering above. I woke with a feeling that the ancient tree had imbued in me a knowledge I couldn't understand. A voiceless voice whispering in my unconscious. But like a willo-the-wisp that knowledge is there somewhere. It's just to the right of me, then to the left. Above me, below me. Behind me, but never, ever right there in front of me. If I pretend not to look I can sometimes catch it in the corner of my eye. Like a lost memory that dances on the tip of my tongue. Invariably though it is always faster than me. I am always seeking. Searching for something that I don't know I'm searching for.

I remember: it was summer time, but late into August. The earlier midsummer madness of too much light making us crazy had been replaced with the sadder, longer nights, later mornings, a chill in the air and wet dewy dawns. The knowledge of the autumns fast approach was in everything, with winter following for sure, hard on autumns melancholic golden heels. Creating its own drive; to have one last swim in the river, one last lazy stolen day of heat, it also made us lethargic and sleepy. Everywhere there were signs of summers last gasp; faded blooms, plants are overgrown and leggy. Only the roses were still in their element. I love the way roses will endure, through all of winters hardships. If a rose is kept deadheaded it will keep producing blooms. A stark reminder that cutting back and pruning is essential for growth.

That August were staying at the Birnam House Hotel, gearing up for another night of Highland Welcome: Scottish hospitality, the hotel staff forever welcoming and enduring in their understanding. This is what we do. We play wild and beautiful music, dance to ease our souls and drink unfeasible amounts of alcohol. Another night held. A night of friends, old and new, brought together by an event. We fill ourselves. We meet, unplanned, at planned events. We renew and we cherish each other. We find new soul mates, recognised in a tune or song, a grin and a nod, a conversation, and we renew old ties. We invent each other – the best we could possibly be, all deficits gone, seeing only the best in each other. We howl-at-the-moon, we sing-to-the-sun and we cry for the beauty and the tragedy we find in life. We swim in the unity of opposites. We were raucous that night, wild, driven by a full moon, the waning summer heat and the knowledge that time was moving much too quickly. Tick.

I will always treasure these memories; the night spent in The Admirals old battered red van, which was just about big enough to fit twenty folk inside, a sub-party, broken away from the main event. Cosy, intimate and deeply in love for a while, we were parked up outside the back of the Birnam Hotel. Shut away from the night and the townsfolk, who were tucked up in their beds, probably contemplating how to either sleep through the racket or notify the police without being dragged into late night troubles themselves. We all joined in together singing Police songs and joyously declared ourselves; *"So lonely! So lonely! So lonely! So lonely! So lonely! So lonely...well someone told me yesterday...But I just can't convince myself, I couldn't live with no-one else..."* We were blessed to be able to experience real comradeship. Fuelled by excess no doubt, but all the same real and all the same, very necessary. Perhaps that's all the Birnam Oak was trying to tell me; to understand the differences between being alone, being lonely, being a loner and to know the ultimate destruction of loneliness, to the self, as it eats away at the very heart of a person. Turning a good soul cynical and sad by twisting thought and feeling. A thousand years is a long time to stand in one place, rooted, fixed, and observe a changing world. How terribly sad to be the last one. To be the only one. To be a Lonesome George

Chapter 7

Repetition – *the action or an instance of repeating.*

'...
...........................'

'There's a moth rattling at the mesh…I am a part in dreams…'

November and '*these dreams of you….'*

Every night I dream. I sleep just under the waking point, surfing a fine line between waking and slumber, with lines of songs spinning round and round in my ear, ear worms that are repeating and repeating and repeating. They torture me, these songs, with their insistence and their true hold over me. They shape my past, they are my future. They colour my present. And every night I dream the same dreams, over and over they come to me and I wake up in fright as once more I fall.

In one of these dreams I am in a white room but there is too much light and it's hard to see. There is too little definition. The scene is like a photograph; overdeveloped or left too long in the sun, it is bleached and patchy. I am with a woman who is known to me only as Delilah. The dream begins with me watching her sleep. I am waiting, watchful and tense. She wakes and hears me and then all hell breaks loose. I flee from her rage. I wander through neon lit familiar streets with a white fog trailing me and leaving wet prints on all it touches. I cannot bear my loneliness and eventually I return to the white room. Then we are talking in low, hushed, sad tones. Our voices betray us. They show the strain, the hardness, the grief that surrounds us. We are brittle, like old dry cellophane, like the bones of the ancient, like yellowed newspaper used to line the bottom drawer of a chest of drawers, a trousseau from pre – war days. The cold and deep anger that we feel toward each other is palpable and so thick it creates solid air, ugly and real, and the knowledge one of us must leave very soon hangs between us like a sharp and ready axe. Is it you or is it me?

In my sleep I struggle, unconsciously wrapping the bedclothes tighter around myself, thereby furthering my anxiety and my fear and I badly want to cry out, to make it known I am hurting. My heart feels much too big for my body and I have a physical pain in my solar plexus that makes it hard to breathe. My hair is sticky around my neck and face. In my dreamtime Delilah's face is ashen. Her voice hardly raised above a throaty croak.

"How did you?" She asks. Her eyes are bright and hard, her breathing ragged and irregular. Her gaze insistent. I try to avoid her question. I try to avoid her eyes, they are beautiful, gold flecked and angry. I know I can't avoid her accusation, but I try never-the-less. I need more time. I need to keep her near. I need her. I need.

"David told me," I eventually reply quietly. My heart is breaking. Simple. And oh so quiet. You would think a broken heart would tear and rip and be heard throughout the universe, after all its breaks the fabric of time as it distorts and bends all feeling. It polarizes and reduces life to a single thought, a single emotion. It is crushing in its absolutes and in breaking it leaves nothing but itself and in doing so feeds only itself. Waves of dark keep creeping over me, starting in the centre of my ribs and rippling slowly out; a stone dropped in still black water. No more would I.

"He had no right!" she flashes at me. Getting angry now. Getting scared.

"He had no choice." I murmur. Suddenly, crushingly, tired.

Then it all goes black again. I hear a buzzing. I am falling. Spinning. Space stretches out around me and I am only aware of how far I am falling. I wake again frightened and alone. I fall back to sleep exhausted by my dreams, and they begin over again, accompanied always by the soundtracks of my years.

I dream I am travelling, perhaps in time, I cannot say. The landscape is awesome, mighty, massive and oh so bleak; peat bogs, cliffs, huge seabirds. The sea is all colours of green and the waves are white and foaming, some are filled with sand that the rolling surf has churned from the sea bed. I can see no life there, apart from the seas own deep and mysterious soul, which breathes and booms. I can see no boat. The sky is rippled with white clouds, and through the spaces in the torn clouds layered one on the other, stacking high into the stratosphere, the original blue shows in deep swathes. It is dawn and the wind is roaring. The sea roars back. I believe it is dawn, but it is hard to be sure. The light is intense, northern Scotland around midsummer perhaps. Who knows? It bothers me deeply that I cannot place the season. I don't know why. I wonder if I am in the Shetland Isles, or Lewis, another place, another time. Somewhere held dear in my memory. I am arguing with someone, a bitter confrontation, but I cannot see them. I can only hear their voice, which is removed in the same way ones own voice is peculiar but familiar on a recording; diction and intonation changed by being outside your own head. Changed by your own ears and brain processing sounds. We rage at one another, this Other and I, we rage along the barren cold coastline, pushing and pulling. I push. I pull. And then I am falling. I fall. Thirty two feet per second.

In waking life, in those moments when I am truly awake and can say with certainty that I am present and true, I try to make sense of the spinning kaleidoscope of feelings and flavours. I cannot work the dreams out and finally, in frustration and desperation, tired of the struggle, worn out with seeking resolution to a circular situation, I decide I must be ranting with myself. Who else can it be? There is no-one here but me. I find I truly cannot bear to not know myself any longer. Tenet Nosce; know thyself. It is part of our humanness, in fact one of the very things that makes us human, this desire to know. The need for comprehension. The craving for cognizance. The need to be known.

No matter what happens, it seems, time tick tocks on. Time will not wait. Although it moves so slowly, imperceptibly forward, it does not stop. Present day follows present day, weeks follow weeks and months creep by and I must decide. I cannot live out my life in a lavender room, I must move on. I must leave. For want of a better explanation I finally decide. When I do my relief is monumental, however, it is only equal to my despair. Hand in hand they sit. Like old friends, like the scales of justice – and I can't seem to have one without the other. Balance. Opposites. But there must be a tipping point. And so I decide, my name is Delilah. It's a good a name as any although I can't work out who David is, or what he's told me. What he's told Delilah.

Epilogue

<u>Revelation – *the revealing of something previously unknown.*</u>

She moves like water, she drifts through endless time. Not enough room at the inn. It turns out there was only room for one. At first the companionship had suited, eventually though the other had become the only. So she had to go, but go where? If not here then where? She drifts through time. Not enough room at the inn. She is cold and tired of searching

The tunes are played, faster and louder, and the beer and whisky are flowing and my tears, held back for all these years seem to never stop. Archie Macdonald has gone to fetch David; he never comes to the pub anymore and typically has no phone. When David arrives, he looks older and sadder. The cold November wind seems to physically push him in through the door. I can see his reluctance to be here; it comes off him in waves, like the Edinburgh Haar which leaves a cold wet print on all it touches. I shiver. I push past the others until I am in standing in front of him.

"Hello Delilah" he says, and then he asks "are you alone?"

Notes

'*Time (The Revelator)*' Gillian Welch.

'*These dreams of you*' Van Morrison.

'the rope of memory' Randall Stevenson, *Modernist Fiction, an Introduction*, Prentice Hall; 1998.

Kierkegaard

'and we run and we run to catch up with the sun…' Pink Floyd.

'How could it have come to this…' World Party.

'I remember holding on to you…was I just of somewhere…' Steve Earle.

'*I'm sitting here burning daylight…*' The Cowboy Junkies.

'*and if a hundred million light years could spiral inward and bend…*' Sharon King.

'so lonely…well someone told me yesterday…' The Police.

A Highland Welcome. Rabbie Burns

'*There's a moth rattling at the mesh, I am a part in dreams.*' Ali McInnis.

About the author

Sharon King is an author, musician, singer and songwriter. Information can be found at http://www.sharonkingmusic.co.uk

She enjoys time travel, cooking, walking, the west coast of Scotland, travelling abroad, staying up late and talking nonsense and lives in Edinburgh with her husband Jasper and cat Frank. She has one grown up daughter.

Re-fraction is her first novella, she is currently working on her first full length novel.

With special thanks

To Jasper King, Rani, Pat, Dave, Mike and Mark Bolam for always supporting me, even when it's a crazy plan.

Thanks also to

To Sue Collins, Ailidh Morrison, Dave and Marion Pope, Heather MacLeod, Heather and Donald MacDougall, Mike and Jude Goddard, Roy and Lindsey Popham, Mary Macmaster, Donald Hay, Lindsey Black and Ali McInnes, Colin Bartie, Jan Crawford and Catriona Ross; for reading my scribbles and encouraging me always.
Kit Bailey, Megan, Geof and Kate King, Wes and Maggie Fyffe, The Reckless Angels, past and present. To the Loch Tay Ladies: Suzy, Jenni, Heather, Dawn, Elspeth, Lenka, Lou and our Mim; for the crazy times, family ties and friendship. To all the Edinburgh girls and boys and in the wider world, who

have kept me grounded and kept me saner. To the Edinburgh party posse – yes we do! My musical community – far and wide, much loved and too many to mention here. Finally, to all the other folk, along the varied roads, who have touched my life in so many ways and helped shape me and fed my creativity. Thank you.

35006019R00041

Made in the USA
Charleston, SC
25 October 2014